HALAL lOVE STORIES

Firdos Tarannum

ISBN 978-93-5610-546-1

Published in India 2022 by Pencil

A brand of
One Point Six Technologies Pvt. Ltd.
123, Building J2, Shram Seva Premises,
Wadala Truck Terminal, Wadala (E)
Mumbai 400037, Maharashtra, INDIA
E connect@thepencilapp.com
W www.thepencilapp.com

DISCLAIMER: *This is a work of fiction. Names, characters, places, events and incidents are the products of the author's imagination. The opinions expressed in this book do not seek to reflect the views of the Publisher.*

Author biography

Firdos Tarannum is a housewife and a mother, who recently inspired herself to write the books after finding her love towards studies, she loved reading and was always appreciated for her work either for her teaching of 3 years or a councilling sessions.

With her support of her spouse she now balances her work, child and book writing.

If one loves something truly then it is the sole responsibility of oneself to take care of surroundings and their talent as well while fulfilling all their responsibilities.

CONTENTS

Foreword

THE original idea was to share my talent of writing to the world, these stories when i shared were very much appreciated thus motivating me to write them in a book format so that the reader can not only read but can also share them.

Preface

Youngsters who usually live in fantasized world of stories this book is such a work where author has tried to put her imagined stories in a beautiful way.

This book is a combination of fantasy stories among most are written by author while the other three stories are real ones with the change in the original names.

This book is just for reading for the one who loves to read stories these stories were written years before which are now getting published in written form.

Hope the reader enjoys the stories.

Acknowledgements

This book doesnt support any kind of religious rulings on these stories, as the names used here are the favourite ones of author, without hurting the sentiments and emotions of any other or respective religious rulings.

Introduction

This book is a purely fictious,

Every person at a certain age gets influenced by surroundings and starts to live in his own world of fantasy to escape the reality.

One among them is author who before marriage thought Everything as a romantic part although the reality is very different and romance in a marriage is just a part but not whole of it.

The author has written these stories in her early teens which she wants to save as a printed format.

PRIDE HIJAB

In marriage, where everyone were busy in work Azaan was the cousin of bridegroom was also busy in shifting gifts from car to bride's room.when he was shifting he heard a sound of sobbing but he couldn't find anyone when he returned he heard it again & then he saw a girl with hijab. in other room named fateen, She was crying in sujood for being insulted, for she was wearing hijab in a gathering , his eeman didn't let him to go near her so, he barely heard a dua from her side.she was asking Allah constantly to grant her a husband who encourage her to wear hijab" hearing this azaan left the place.

Azaan often made same dua which he heard. After couple of for months, he saw her in marriage album and managed to convince.

his parents to marry her

on the day of marriage. Azaan was mesmerised by her beauty as she was still in hijab even on the day of reception, Azaan got ready to attend guests thus left the home quickly.

fateen was also ready but her in laws approached her and forced her not to wear hijab. azaan's sister noticed this and informed azaan, As Soon as Azaan came to knew, he left towards the room & saw fateen in Same situation he saw her for the first time, he grabbed her hand and took her to another room & said,

"Dear fateen, this is the room where i heard your dua for the first time & now it is the time to get it fulfilled, no matter what people say never give up on your hijab because,

YOUR HIJAB IS MY PRIDE

LUCKY MAN

A guy who was a believer of friendship used to drop & pick her sister every week from islamic classes. Once when her sister told her brother that she learnt about friendship, his brother. asked her all about what she learnt, out of curiosity he started to read the notes given in classes about friendship

He became so intrested that every week her -sister used to share topics of clam & the guy used to read notes & even verses of Quran mentioned .

A year passed the same way and his family noticed a huge change in him.

And finally he was on the path of religious guidance and thus his family got him married to a pious girl. Months after his marriage, when he asked his sister the reason for not going to islamic classes anymore, she replied that the girl got married his brother said in his heart, lucky is the man who married her.

his sister asked, "can you ask your wife when will she start classes?" he asked stunningly "why will she take classes &, of about what!".. she said, "o my dear brother, she is the one who used to teach me"

The boy got tears in his eyes and he bowed down thanking Allah that,

HE WAS THE LUCKIEST MAN

THE CHAIN

It was a rushy day for Ahmed as he was getting late to pick her sister from islamic classes, he waited for a while & suddenly he heard the voice of a girl who was teaching students about DUA and she concluded her class by saying,

DUA CAN CHANGE YOUR LIFE

The girl left class but on her way her chain fell down and ahmed noticed it, he picked chain & before he could return she left, As it was last day of class & no one knew much about that girl, so he kept the chain with him. his mind always questioned about how can dua change life? As he was not practicing muslim so, he went islamic scholars to know about dua.

soon, Ahmed learned all about islam and now was a practicing muslim. he often used to make dua for that girl whose words stuck his mind,

months later he was married. when his wife was arranging her clothes she noticed chain and asked her husband about it and he replied "you know what, this chain belongs to that girl who changed my life her by her speech" . his wife handed the same chain & Ahmed looked at her surprisingly, she said 'months before i came here for a guest lecture & often made dua for chain as it was the last gift from my mother'. they boyh happily said

"DUA CAN CHANGE YOUR LIFE

FLIRTING MAN TO PIOUS MAN

A teenaged muslim guy had fake girl's account, he used to flirt with girls by his own written poems, he sent these poems to a muslim girl for one week she didn't replied but one day finally she accepted his friend request thinking that the girl was her classmate.

But when he revealed his identity her reply surprisingly shocked him, she said "be satisfied for how beautifully you are created, As you're created by ALLAH, your poem's come good but it would be very good if you use it in positive way": He was surprised because many of girls would either insult him or block him but this girl neither did these instead praised his poems, he felt so ashamed that he left social media on his own very soon he understood the advise of girl, And he started to write islamic poems.

Within a year his all writings & nasheeds got good name & fame, After a couple of months he opened an account with his real name.

Then he searched the girl's account and went her home to ask her hand for marriage and they got married.

after their marriage, the girl asked him ' why haven't you asked any questions to me before marriage nor enquired about any qualification even once'? He replied ' i knew your qualification of deen, when you messaged me last time, and years ago someone said,

*be satisfied for how beautifully you are create*d

she remembered that he was one, then they both thanked Allah and lead a happy life.

PATIENCE and love

Rabiya was a teenage girl who was about to marry, Like every other girl she too had many expectations about her husband specially going out for a ride walk, shopping.. etc. she was pious girl As soon as she got married, she came to know that the one she married was not a practicing Muslim and there was not even a single sin which he did not committed, he committed every major sin from shirk to zina. Every sin of her husband gave her life a chance to leave him, but she never thought of leaving him. Last time when she came out of her home as a couple was only the next day of her marriage.After a couple of years by her prayers ALHAMDULILLAH her husband changed in such a beautiful way that each day is Iman increased a level up.. but the thing which never changed.

but the thing which never changed in her life was going out with her husband as a couple..Things changed and soon she became a mother of 5 children now she started to travel with her sons.

she used to attend all family functions alone, whenever she was out her husband gave her the money to spend but she always expected the support of him but not money...Time has changed and today is a grandmother and now she travels with her grandchildren.. This is the 43rd year of her marriage and guess what?? After a lot of patience, she is now going out happily as a couple to the world's beautiful place - Mecca for Umrah.

PURPOSE OF LIFE

A guy went to aqua park with his friends, where he noticed a girl who was in hijab. Though he was a muslim but never knew about haya, the girl didn't entered pool as park had swimming costumes & hijab was not allowed.

she denied to play games where hijab was not allowed, she just sat at corner watching her cousins play.

The guy silently noticed all her actions when one of her cousin asked her about not being involved in pool, she replied "if i used to remove hijab, why would have weared it ,

There is a purpose for everythig coming into your life.'

Her cousin asked 'but you'll miss all the enjoyement she said "am enjoying by being slave of Allah" The boy stood stunned at her reply & went back, all the way to home there were many questions running in his mind like "she didn't even looked at me am i not good enough, what was the purpose of her coming into my life?' & what he is HAYA" he was so stressed out.

He went to masjid to pray before he could come out he was stopped by hearing an announcement of speech which was about haya thus he heard it a came and to knew all about it, he felt guilty that the girl maintained her haya but he didn't.

Later, he thanked Allah for guidance a repented for his sins. he often made dua for that girl whose entry in his life gave a purpose for him to live. soon, he started practicing deen & now he was a practicing muslim.

Months later, he was invited in a youth program to share his inspiring story. At the end there was questions session, Suddenly he heard the voice of the same girl. soon he got her address & asked her hand for marriage and finally they got married & lived happily.

THE AZAAN MAN

fatima was a pious girl, she loved to attend islamic lectures, once when she attended an islamic youth program, there she she heard Azan, she was mesmerized by the voice of one calling for prayer she answered azaan And made dua that "Allah i want my husband to have a voice like him..." she made Same dua for 10 days.

Months passed by and she forgot the dua, Many marriage proposals came & were rejected, it was 9th proposal, fatima performed istikhara and the answer was YES. though her parents didn't wanted her to marrry due to his poor earnings but she convinced them to have belief in Allah's decision

she married him & two days after their marriage they were on their way back to home after performing a ritual. fatima was still unknown of reason for getting married to him, her husband" said, "i have bought a gift for you" before he could give her gift, he stopped the vehicle and went away for prayer. fatima was still sad & suddenly she heard same voice of azaan which she heard months ago.

she rushed to masjid and prayed calmly came out of masjid, she saw her husband coming out after prayer.

she asked her husband who gave the azaan?" her husband said "As there was no one, so i gave the azaan, wait let me just bring the gift"

fatima grabbed his hand, & said "you know what,

Allah has given me the most beautiful gift"

then she narrated the whole story, they went back running towards masjid, & performed the prayer and thanked Allah.

FORGIVE ME

Aysha was a strict maintainer of haya & hijab who studies in topmost medical co-education college Ahmed was also studying in same college. On the day of a college function ,Ahmed's friend challenged him to talk to her out of curiosity he accepted. on day of fresher's party, he went on stage and started screaming her name forcing her to come out.

Ahmed bent on his knee & asked her "o Aysha, will you be my friend?" Aysha with in hesitation - with modesty she replied

"if you answer me then i will do whatever you say, Tell me the exact time of judgement day" Ahmed stood stunned feeling insulted & decided to answer her in revenge, Aysha left the place in tears,

After a week Ahmed gained knowledge about it realised that he was wrong and thus returned to college to apologise aysha

but left himself of guilty as aysha left the college forever after the incident, years later, ahmed was settled as a pious muslim ,and often repented for his mistake on the other hand Ahmed's mother wanted him to get married, and he later got married,

Just before the last ritual of marriage; he was waiting for his bride as as saw the bride,he ran towards holding her hand saying "o Aysha forgive me" Aysha heard the voice and knew it was Ahmed's. she said, "o Ahmed,i forgive you"

, Ahmed asked "o Aysha, will you be my friend". this time she replied with excitement 'yes yes forever" everyone around shouted Mashallah.

INTERNET FRIENDS

Shahid and shifa were internet friends.when shifa came to know that it was haram she left texting him & shahid asked her multiple times for no longer response of messages.

shifa advised him to ask an islamic scholar about the sin & shahid did it accordingly. upon realising he was guilty that he commited a sin .shahid left her & concentrated solely on his work, soon he was settled in his life, whenever his parents approached him for marriage, his mind always stinged about shifa

when one fine day he reached masjid in confused state where he heard a Statement that

whatever is meant you will reach you no matter what

shahid took a month time before marriage " packed his bag left the place in a Search of shifa.

Though he reached the place but wasn't aware of her address, so he stayed in masjid for 3 days. A residing muslim there accepted him as a guest & took him to his home.

shahid lived there for 28 days, on 28th day, he packed his bag out of despair to go back, but the man who noticed him to be a righteous person asked his hand for his daughter.

when shahid heard the daughter's name to be shifa, he rushed to pray with fear and hope. he . took permission to atleast see her once. Atlast when they met shifa requested "aren't you shahid'

shahid was so relieved with joy & bent. down without even looking at her saying for sure what was meant me has reached me.

RESPECT EACH OTHER

A muslim couple lead a happy life with their 6 year old daughter.. When her wife was pregnant for second time she faced a miscarriage... But months later, she was expecting again. After 3 months of pregnancy she was advised of complete bedrest for 6 months.

The only thing for which she was feared of was about taking care of husband and child who were alone.

Soon she gave birth to girl child, everything seemed happy but her happiness didn't longed.. Just after 40 days of child birth Her internal stitches loosened and caused a big infection and severe pain to her..She told her husband about the pain but never showed any seriousness about it... All that mattered for her was to be with her husband and children happily in her own home.

Her husband was not aware of pain she was going through. He used to take her near doctor for checkup he helped her financially but never asked her about pain.One day asusual when they went for checkup she told her husband to stay there.. When her infection was shown to him he was heartbroken and this all happened within 4 months.He hugged her and cried as he was feeling guilty.Her major operation was carried out to clean infection in ramzan which took 2 months and 1 month for her recovery. At every step of her life her husband not only took care of her but also managed the studies of first child and care of 6 months baby.Love is not just to share your wardrobe, room or feelings. It is even to share responsibilities of each other.

CRAZY GIRL

Suheb was riding his bike on high speed In all of sudden he tried to control his bike so hard to save himself from accident

he stopped his bike because, of a girl who came infront of his bike to help an old woman to cross the road, he angrily yelled at her, "are you crazy?" and left the place.

Next day, while he was passing by the same place he remembered the incident & said "what a crazy girl was she & he saw her in a nearby hotel on the same road with same old lady'

After few days, he saw her again where she paid the bill the left place hurriedly leaving the old lady there,

After reaching there he ordered for himself and sat near the lady, After, his breakfast he asked the lady politely "shall i drop you somewhere?"

The old lady replied 'where will i go?'. suheb interrupted 'what about the girl, isn't your daughter?;

The old lady with the tears answered.'i wish she was, she is good human among bad people, she comes here daily helps me to cross the road, takes me to this hotel for breakfast pays the bill and leaves the place' he said in his heart 'o man! she is really crazy' he wanted to know more about but only got to know that she lives in a nearby place.. however he later managed to find thevcomplete information'. and was also succesful in convincing his family for their marriage.

on the day of marriage suhaib's cousin teased him by saying 'what do you say about your wife ,brother.?" He said

"She is a crazy girl but Alhamdulillah that she is mine now"

DAWAH CONNECTION

Simran was going back to home from college on her way where she had an accident. with a car though she was safe but hey Scooty[vehicle] was badly damaged, before the car driver could apologise she left the place, the car driver informed to owner, shafi regarding the matter who was a school manager and a practising muslim.

the following day, they both waited at the place to compensate but simran couldn't notice them as she was in rush, s0 shafi followed her till she reached a small school

shafi entered the school and found her to be busy in teaching about religion, so he thought not to disturb her & thus waited in office room.

However he managed to have good conversation with principal as they were from same profession. A while later.

he explained whole matter to principal and handed a cheque and said "I'm waiting here to compensate for the damage done to her vehicle but thanks to Allah that came to know that she is a hard working girl who reads and teaches, earlier i wanted to compensate but now i want to help her':

principal asked ;what help" He replied; i know it's tough to manage So,...' the principal interuppted by saying 'she is not in need of it, she teaches here as she is intrested in teaching religion, without expecting a single penny"

shafi was surprised and after few days he managed to take the permission of her guardian for marriage. Now both are happily married, where, simran teaches in school after all

it's dawah connection.

HELP YOU

shoib was appointed as an organiser of shop in exhibition, shaziya visited with her friends she entered the shop but wasn't aware of prices. shoib saw her & understood that she needed. help & asked "shall help you?" she replied, "actually yes". before leaving the shop, her toe hit the table & started bleeding

shoib said," let me just help you?' she asked for some cotton, but there wasn't so he gave his handkerchief., she thanked and the left place

Shoib often used to make dua as he was quite impressed by her modesty, whenevre his mom handed him photos for marriage he asusual used to ignore her.

a few days later, shoib recieved a call from manager that he needs to take payment from a particular address.

He reached the place, after taking the amount, the house owner asked him to wait. she said.'when i visited your (shop) shop last time one of your worker helped me, i think his name starts with s as it has print on it, please thank him and return this (kercief).'.Shoib was extremely happy, he rushed back home and explained the story to his mom and finally married her on day of marriage. shaziya was crying shoib wiped her tears and handed the handkerchief, shaziya slipped before entering into car he asked her politely "shall i help you?'

This left her confused she then slowly opened the kerchief Looking at letter 's' she looked at him surprisingly and they both winked.

SOUL MATES

Rehmat and abid were school mates, same school n class.. As soon as school time ended, abid entered into college life and rehmat was married, she soon became a mother of 2 children..

And her husband died, now she was a single parent, she was a brave girl.. Time passed by and there abid.

And here abid was also happily married and soon became a proud father, even his happiness didn't last long.It became hard to manage business and to look after kids without mother..

Rehmath on other side, worked hard to look after her children, she got married her daughter and managed to get a good job in foreign for her son.Though now she was free but she was alone,.. Abid faced same thing.Every one of their loved ones became so busy, time passed by today they are grandparents, though they had a smile on their face for a while, but every second was getting tough to be alone in home for them..Abid's children were of modern thinking and now they wanted abid to get setlle, abid though ignored bec he thought it was not his age to marry again.. But didn't wanted to hurt his kids so, he agreed to go n meet girl.. He was so nervous..

He finally went to meet and he saw rehmath with same fear on her face waiting for him, he had mixed emotions but no nervousness bec they had good comfort level.. They finally approved each other for marriage..

Even today whenever i see them dnt see a couple i just see two good friends calling nicknames of school time, free of every responsibility, just sitting and sharing their past memories, walking and laughing together.. Mashallah

This is their awesome journey from SCHOOLMATE TO SOULMATE

Notes

this book has no extra volumes, while any other further addition of stories are updated only on author's social media accounts namely

nabi_e_ummah

charge_ur_eemaan

www.ingramcontent.com/pod-product-compliance
Lightning Source LLC
La Vergne TN
LVHW050428160726
843469LV00041B/1280

* 9 7 8 9 3 5 6 1 0 5 4 6 1 *